Red Berry Wool

Robyn Eversole
PAINTINGS BY Tim Coffey

Albert Whitman & Company
Morton Grove, Illinois

IN A MEADOW on a mountain near the town, a boy watched over a flock of sheep.

The smartest lamb was called Lalo. He noticed everything. One day, he noticed something different about the Boy.

“Why is the Boy bright like berries?” Lalo asked his mother.

“That’s his sweater,” Lalo’s mother said. “Isn’t it lovely? It’s made from our wool.”

Other boys in town wore shiny, zippered jackets with words on the back. But not the Boy. He wore a warm, berry-colored, sheep-wool sweater instead.

Made from our wool, thought Lalo. He looked at his wool in the drinking pond. But it was straggly, and muddy, and full of bits of straw. He wished that it could be a sweater. Then he would look splendid like the Boy.

"How does wool become a sweater?" Lalo asked his mother.

"Well," said his mother, "let me think." She thought hard. A long time ago, she had been a lamb in the yard of the big house, and she had seen this done.

"I remember," she said.

"First, you wash the wool.

Then you spin it.

Then you dye the wool.

Then — you knit it."

Lalo walked across the meadow, repeating to himself:

Wash the wool.
Spin it.
Dye the wool.
Knit it,

so that he would not forget.

Washing came first. Lalo went down to the drinking pond and waded in.

Tadpoles tickled his legs, and the water was cold. He did not like water slosh-sloshing around his knees. But he had to wash his wool before it could become a sweater like the Boy's.

Lalo waded in deeper. Then he stepped on a rock—and slipped. His legs went up. His nose went down.

"Baaaaa!" Lalo cried. "Help!"

Water was in his nose. It was in his eyes. It was everywhere it shouldn't be.

"Help!" cried Lalo.

And the Boy came running.

He lifted Lalo and held him close. Then he dried him off and sat beside him in the warm sun, stroking him until he stopped trembling.

From now on, thought Lalo, *the drinking pond's just for drinking.*

But his wool was washed. When Lalo felt better, he remembered what he had to do:

Wash the wool.
Spin it.
Dye the wool.
Knit it.

Spinning came next. Lalo went off to the far corner of the meadow, where no one would see him. And then he began to do a strange, very un-lamblike thing.

He turned around and around like a dog does before napping. He turned faster and faster, until the meadow was a blur and he was spinning.

He didn't like spinning. It made him dizzy. But he had to spin his wool so it could become a sweater like the Boy's.

Lalo spun and spun, out to the end of the meadow where the ground sloped down and the rocks cropped up.

Lalo spun all the way over the slope...

…and down and down, hooves over ears, to a low place and a thorn bush. Ouch.

"Baaaaa!" cried Lalo. "Help!"

He had a bump on his head and thorns in his tail, and he didn't know where he was.

"Help!" Lalo cried.

And the Boy came running.

The Boy slid down the slope, scraping his hands on the rocks. He scooped up Lalo and carried him back to the meadow.

Then he plucked the thorns from Lalo's tail and sat with him in the sun, holding him until everything stopped spinning.

I didn't mean to spin the whole meadow, too, thought Lalo.

But his wool was spun now. He was halfway done! Soon he would have a sweater just like the Boy's.

Wash the wool.
Spin it.
Dye the wool.
Knit it,

Lalo repeated to himself.

"What is *dyeing* wool?" Lalo asked his mother.

She looked up from her grass. "Dyeing? That means changing wool's color. Instead of white like sheep, it turns green like meadows, or blue like pond water."

"Or red like berries?" asked Lalo.

"Or red like berries," said Lalo's mother.

Lalo knew where to find berries. Last week, the Boy had taken the flock to another meadow, full of berry bushes. Lalo was sure he remembered how to go:

Down a valley and up a valley,
along a long road,
past a forest.

Lalo set off. He went down a valley and up a valley, all by himself.

Lalo walked along the long road, past the forest, to the other meadow. The bushes were filled with red berries, just the color he wanted his wool to be.

Lalo stepped in among the berries. First he ate some, but his wool didn't get any redder that way. So Lalo lay down on top of the berry bushes. He rolled back and forth, back and forth, to let the juice make his wool berry-red.

But Lalo rolled onto a snake by mistake. The snake bit hard into his leg.

"Baaaaa!" Lalo cried. "Ouch! Help!"

Lalo couldn't get up. His leg felt huge, and his head filled up with fog.

"Help!" he cried over and over, but the Boy was a long way off—down a valley and up a valley—and how could he ever hear that far?

Still, Lalo called “Help!”

…and following lamb-tracks in the damp earth, the Boy came.

He gathered up Lalo. He found the place where the snake had bit and drew the poison out with his own mouth. Then the fog went away from Lalo's eyes, and his leg stopped feeling the size of a cart and only stung a little.

Then the Boy carried Lalo back, along a long road, down a valley and up a valley to home.

Lalo had washed and spun and dyed his wool. He couldn't wait to see it, new and beautiful—and berry-red.

But when Lalo looked into the drinking pond, his wool was even uglier and more straggly than before. It was full of burrs. It wasn't berry-red, either. It just had brownish splotches where the berries had stained it.

I must have done everything wrong, thought Lalo.
He sat down beside the drinking pond, miserable.
I will never look splendid like the Boy.

The Boy sat down, too. He stroked Lalo's wool as if he didn't care about the burrs and the splotches. He stroked Lalo's wool as if it were as smooth and bright as his own sweater.

Then Lalo remembered that there was one last step to making a sweater—one thing that he had forgotten to do. *Knit the wool.*

Lalo found his mother on the far side of the meadow. "What does *knit* mean?" he asked her.

"Knit? Let me think." Lalo's mother thought for five whole mouthfuls of grass.

At last she said, "Knit means to bring things together."

So Lalo went back to the drinking pond and the Boy. *Now I'm not going anywhere*, Lalo thought. *Now we are together.*

The Boy told Lalo a brave-sheep story. Lalo showed him a new lamb leap. Then they sat and watched the sunset stretch from mountain to mountain, turning their whole meadow berry-red.

For my mom. —R. E.

To my mom and dad, who supported me
in my struggle to become an artist. —T. C.

Eversole, Robyn Harbert.
Red berry wool / by Robyn Eversole ; illustrated by Tim Coffey.
p. cm.
Summary: Lalo the lamb wants to have a bright sweater like the one
the shepherd boy wears, but Lalo has a very hard time washing,
spinning, and dyeing his own wool.
ISBN 0-8075-0654-0
[1. Sheep — Fiction. 2. Wool — Fiction. 3. Shepherds — Fiction.]
I. Coffey, Tim, ill. II. Title.
PZ7.E9235Rg 1999 [E] — dc21 99-10696
CIP

Published in 1999 by Albert Whitman & Company,
6340 Oakton Street, Morton Grove, Illinois 60053-2723.
Published simultaneously in Canada by
General Publishing, Limited, Toronto.

Printed in the United States of America.
10 9 8 7 6 5 4 3 2

The paintings are rendered in acrylic on watercolor paper textured with gesso.
The design is by Scott Piehl.